# Runaway Bride

*A Titillating, Feel-Good Romance Tale of Betrayal and the Reunion of Long-Lost Love*

By

**BILL WILSON**

# Table of Contents

# Chapter One

It was a cool evening, the gentle breeze from outside billowed the curtains at contact. The windows were wide open as Sarah Meyers was enjoying the weather. Their small downtown house was exceptionally silent. Not that it was always noisy; at least quiet is maintained when her Father is not around. Everyone else had gone out to do a thing or two, mother to the market and then the store, father had gone to work, John to play with his friends and Joan to one of her classes.

"This is really a good time to read one of those novels I got from Anna since no one is at home," Sarah thought to herself. Anna was her childhood friend who often supplied her with breathtaking romance novels. She often hid these books from her family because she wouldn't want them to have the wrong opinion of her. It was like living in bondage, but that's the best for her for now.

Sarah reached for her bag that was kept underneath her bed. She had kept it there in such a way that it wouldn't draw anyone's attention. The bag contained her valuables and secrets; she kept her daily dairy and novels there. She brought out this bag and then laid back on her bed again, locked the door and got set to sail away into the world of books.

This particular novel was about a wolf boy who experiences forbidden love by falling in love with the pastor's daughter. Ideally nobody must know about their affair so he came to visit only at night when everyone was asleep. Their affair went on for a while until she asked him to come on a full moon night.

The request was inspired by her harmless desire to see what he looked like in his full wolf state. He agreed and appeared the way she wanted. Unknowingly to the both of them they were being watched and the girl's father shot the wolf boy dead. The girl wailed and was scarred for life.

"This is such a terrible terrible tragedy," Sarah thought to herself while throwing the book to the other side of the bed.

"Why does he have to die, he is such a sweet boy. I thought wolves were very strong. After all it's a full Moon, oh my god now I wish I didn't read that," she said feeling a lump form in her throat. Sarah is such an emotional person and she would cry over anything and everything. Despite being the eldest of her parent's children, she is the one who is always crying whenever their parents have their usual argument or whenever she quarreled with her siblings over something.

"I really should have stopped at the parts where their love was rosy. Oh I really enjoyed those parts. Love can be such a sweet sweet thing to experience." Sarah thought, letting her mind drift away from the sad ending of the book to the part she enjoyed the most.

Interestingly, despite the fact that her parent's marriage is a bad example of a marriage, Sarah never for once stopped believing in the concept. She had always held the belief in her heart that there's someone somewhere that is her other half. And that is the person meant for her.

Sarah thought about some scenes in the novel; the part where they went out together for the first time, their first kiss, sex, where he beat up someone else for her and his dying moment in her arms. The dying part aside, she wants something like that, being in love with someone that she wants.

While she was thinking about this, Liam popped up in her mind. Liam was the only son in the family of their next door neighbors. She had only spoken to him for about two or three times, but she sometimes wondered what a relationship with him would feel or look like. She actually doesn't feel okay, thinking this about someone she barely knows, but the problem lies in the fact that she cannot stop herself from thinking it. Anna says that she might have a crush on him, or worst still be infatuated with him.

"I love it when Liam stands close to the window to get dressed. His body is built in such a great way and his psyche makes my heart pound. I love seeing him turn around to smile for his mom whenever he's about to leave — he is such an angel. I like the sound of his voice too and I hope a chance will present itself for us to finally talk.

As much as Sarah is excited about the idea of talking to Liam, she is also scared about it. Anna had said that if they ever talk, there are two possibilities. It is either she stops liking him based on the kind of person he is or she falls even more in love with him. Anna goes on to paint a gory image of her being in love with him and him seeing her as just a friend. All these made Liam scared and she covered her mouth quickly to prevent a scream from escaping.

"It all doesn't matter anyways. We might never ever get to talk to each other and I will forget about him," Sarah told herself.

"Sarah!" The rude voice was followed by a loud bang on the door, it's John. It could be Joan too as there isn't much difference between the two.

"I'm coming, give me a few more minutes," Sarah shouted back at whoever it was that wanted to break down the door to her room. She quickly dragged out her secret bag and returned the novel. She got home and as she made for the door, she could hear only Joan and John.

"These two rarely come into my room at the same time. It was either because they had some news to deliver or they need the services of a mediator," Sarah thought with a face expressing harmless disgust.

"So is there any news or you guys fought over something?" Sarah asked, quite authoritatively.

"Why are you trying so hard to be serious?" Joan asked before bursting into laughter. Sarah was actually an introvert who carried a serious face most times, but her siblings knew how to break through her serious side and make her a little goofy sometimes.

"We didn't fight over anything," Joan said.
"I'd like to hear the same from John just so we can be sure," Sarah objected, expressing her doubt.

"We really didn't fight over anything, what do you take us for really?" John replied trying to stop himself from laughing.

John started, "Father had told us to come inform you…"

"… That our neighbor has invited us for dinner tonight and they will be hosting all of us," an excited Joan completed the sentence for John.

"What neighbors?" Sarah asked just to be sure.

"Liam's family of course. The others couldn't have invited us obviously," John replied

"We will go and get dressed now and father wants you to do the same, we don't want to spend eternity in someone's house."

Both Joan and John went into their room after relaying the message. Sarah  turned to go into her room in disbelief. It was almost as though she was a soothsayer.  She was wishing to have a discussion with Liam and now all of a sudden it's happening. Her feeling of excitement overwhelmed her shock and in no time she was ransacking her bags for her best dress.

She stopped at intervals to play conversations in her head. She imagined what Liam would look like up close, whether he'd be fun to be with, if he was a snob or not. After a long while of deliberating, Sarah finally decided to go for her red dress, which was a gift from her favorite aunt. She loved the dress because of its exceptional floral lace trimmings; it was really a product of an excellent fashionista. She is also very comfortable in the dress.

"I hope Liam likes my dress and compliments it, it will warm my heart so much," Sarah thought.

She walked gracefully down the stairs to join her waiting family. While her mother and Joan and begun complimenting and adjusting her dress, her father, Marcus, sat in silence with irritation written on his face. Sarah didn't pay much attention to this as that had been their father's natural facial expression in the house for years now. Sarah grew up knowing Marcus as a loving father, but since he had lost his job some years ago he had taken a bad turn. Suddenly, the women's business was rudely interrupted by Marcus' voice.

"Do not tell me this is the dress you intend to wear to out host's house?" Marcus asked with obvious anger in his voice.

"Yes dad, this is the dress I wish to wear, it fits me perfectly."

"I do not care, I think you look better in some other dress. So go and change this," Marcus commanded.

Sarah felt bad about her father's statement. She looked at her mother for a defense hoping seriously that she would protest. There was disappointment written on her face, but she felt too much fear to say a word. Sarah waited for a little more before her father's shouting jolted her back to life. She scurried away towards the stairs and into her room.

In her room she was mad at her mother's helplessness. She hated herself even more for not being able to protest her father's choice as being against hers. She became sad about her life and her kind of father.

"Why does it have to be this way, why do I always have to do my father's bidding? I cannot even

wear my preferred dress. What sort of life is this?"
Sarah asked herself alone in her room and close to
tears. Meanwhile her family was waiting downstairs,
and Joan was finally sent to get her. Sarah, who
had been thinking, had almost forgotten about the
outing. When Joan knocked on her door, she
remembered immediately and started looking for a
dress she believed her father would like.

"Sarah..." Joan said coming in. "I know you're upset
about dad's reaction to your choice of dress, I am
also unhappy."

"Oh that, it's really nothing," Sarah said, faking a
smile

"I know it's something, but I believe you if you say
so," Joan added. An awkward silence fell on the
room and the sisters sat staring at each other
before Joan made the move to hug Sarah and
Sarah embraced her in return. Although Sarah was
not the best at expressing herself and she was often
quiet, Joan always managed to see through her.

She loved that about Joan and would always want to gift her things.

Joan and John, "the twins" as Sarah and her parents often called them, were Sarah's siblings. They were born when she was six years old. Their mother often made fun of Sarah for crying bitterly whenever someone mentioned that her mother was having a baby back then. She said the idea of carrying a baby inside terrified Sarah as a child and she even tried poking her mother's stomach to be sure it wasn't just inflated.

The night Sarah's mom went into labor, Sarah knew something was wrong despite being a child. She was credited for her unusual bravery. She ran into the heavy rain that night to call their then neighbors and inform them of her mother's situation. Although she later broke into uncontrollable tears when she realized that her mom would be taken to the hospital without her.

Finally, when Joan and John were delivered, she jumped around in the hospital and placed kisses on the babies' heads as often as she was allowed. Now, they are all grown, with Sarah being 18 years old and the twins were 15 years. Those little babies now had facial hair, broad shoulders and hips, baritone voices and other obvious signs of puberty. How time flies.

Joan also joined Sarah in picking out a dress. Finally, they settled for a dress their dad had gotten for Sarah.

"He should like this one since he got it for you," Joan said.

"I actually don't care what he likes," Sarah replied with anger.

"I know, please let's go downstairs. We are late by now," Joan said, moving towards the door. Sarah left her heap of clothes on the bed and followed Joan.

"I will deal with that when I get back," she thought.

Downstairs, Sarah's family were waiting. Her father was already tapping his foot on the floor in a quite loud and obvious manner, which is what he does whenever he is angry. On seeing Sarah and the dress his face betrayed him as a smile managed to form on his ever frowning face. This was all the approval that was needed.

The anger she was feeling didn't even make her show her changed dress to her father, but the look on his face said it all. He seemed to prefer the dress. All set now, the family got up to take their leave. The Jamesons, which is the name of Liam's family who moved into their neighborhood not long ago and their house is just a short distance away from that of Sarah's family.

Marcus and his wife, Sarah's mother led the way. Joan and John followed them behind chatting away. Aside from their frequent fights the duo always get along well. They have a couple of things in common. They are both expert Scrabble players and would often review their last games together and argue over the rules of the game.

Sarah walked silently behind her family with a lot of thoughts flying around in her head. What would she act like in their host's house? Will Liam be handsome when he is up close? Will the friendly dinner go well without any grudges or fighting? These and more are the things that bothered Sarah while she and her family covered the distance to the Jameson's house on foot.

# Chapter Two

If you are meeting Sarah's family for the first time, it is easy for you to identify their bond. The children look so much alike with each inheriting one trait or feature from each parent. Sarah is the most perfect example. Although a very beautiful girl, she shared some resemblance with her father. She had his kind of nose, and got her impressive height from him as well as some of his cute speech mannerism.

On the other hand, Sarah had gotten some of her mother's beauty genes. Her face was round and perfectly shaped just like her mother's. Her post pubertal breasts are full and even under clothes the roundness announces itself. Her hair is dark, straight and bouncy just like her mother's. Her body shape also qualifies as sexy, especially for her age. She is indeed a beautiful lady overall.

However, Sarah hates it when someone calls her beautiful. Whenever anyone gushes over her beautiful features she gets shy and confused on how to act. She would often stutter and struggle with words like thank you. As a matter of fact, deep down, Sarah never believed anyone who called her beautiful because she thought that they were all lying to her.

The last time someone complimented her and she believed them, it didn't end so well. It was her then friend Robin. They were all just experiencing pubertal changes and he had called her beautiful just to get her to show him her just blooming boobs. She got comfortable as a result of his numerous compliments and showed him. Days later he wouldn't stop talking about it and he even had told a few of his friends. Sarah despised compliments and even boys since then. But since she saw Liam recently, she is scared that that is about to change.

Finally, they all arrived at the Jameson's home. John rang the bell and stepped back waiting for a response. After a while and nobody showed up, he did it again and just when he was about to go for a third time, the door was opened from the back and that startled everyone. When composite was restored, they all laughed about it.

It was Liam's mother who came to answer the door. She had a kitchen apron around her and the smell of cooking and the aroma of food was all over her body. She spread her lips to form a wide smile and hugged Sarah's mother while welcoming her to their home. She also hugged Marcus in a side hug, which was not as tight as the hug she gave Sarah's mom. She also didn't peck him on both cheeks. While all this was going on, the kids stood behind their parents waiting for their chance to finally greet Mrs. Jameson.

"Good evening ma, I am Joan and I love your hair," Joan said, going first.

"Oh really? Thank you very much, yours is also lovely my angel," Mrs. Jameson blushed.

"Good evening Mrs. Jameson," Sarah and John said at the same time.

"Good evening to you too, please forgive me. Can we all come in?" Mrs. Jameson said, opening the door wide so that everyone could come in.

Inside, she led them to the family's sitting room and pointed to the sofas.

"Please have your seats here, I am going to quickly inform the rest of my family of your arrival," Mrs. Jameson said and climbed the stairs, disappearing into the other part of her home.

The apartment is very nice. It is like the conventional homes in the neighborhood. It didn't exactly show wealth, but it looked a little better than that of Marcus's family. The sofas are very comfy and the floor was well polished. Joan pointed to the group pictures on the wall and there was this one that showed Liam  when he was very young. He was wearing a checked shirt and his hair was combed to the side. He looked very cute for a child of his age and wore a very big smile, he must have been so happy on that day.

Marcus called John to order as he tried to reach for the porcelain close to the sofa. The Jamesons followed each other down the stairs. A young girl of Joan and John's age led the way and she was followed by Mr. and Mrs. Jameson, who both wore a very big smile that appeared to be plastered on their faces.

There was no Liam in sight and Sarah's heart sank. She hadn't seen much of him since they moved into their neighborhood. The few times she had met him was when he came to make some inquiries from her parents and so they rarely spoke. She managed to learn his name from when his mother and siblings called for him.

"Can today get any worse? First it was my dad who wouldn't respect my choice. Now Liam is not around or won't come down the stairs," Sarah thought sadly.

When Mr. and Mrs. Jameson got to where Marcus and his family were, they stood up politely to exchange pleasantries. At the end of the hellos, Mr. Jameson started speaking;

"Wow, I'm very pleased and honored to host you and your family. As a matter of fact I'm quite surprised that our invite got honored. This is just our little way of saying thank you for your warm reception when we first moved into this neighborhood." Mr. Jameson said, wiping his face with a handkerchief at the end of his statement.

Marcus sat up, gave a very friendly smile and talked about how it was all nothing and went on to commend the Jameson's thoughtfulness. The two, Marcus and Jameson, went on talking about how the two families should build a bond and from there moved to some other topics. Joan, John and the Jameson's daughter, Robyn had started getting on.

Sarah's mother offered to join Mrs. Jameson in the kitchen and the two women left the gathering. Sarah was on her own, shifting attention from one corner of the room to the other. While at it, she heard a masculine voice over her head.

"Why are you seated all alone? I like your dress, you look beautiful in it." The voice belonged to Liam, who had now entered into the room to join the rest of his family. On seeing him, Sarah became lost for words and she didn't know what to say, yet she wanted to say so many things all at once. In the end she just sat down and stared at Liam.

"No way, there is absolutely no way that Liam sounds like this and look this good. Who would have thought that he would be speaking to me first? My day just took a wonderful turn!" Sarah thought to herself while Liam stood in front of her waiting for a response. As Liam turned to leave Sarah's presence, she spoke,

"Oh hi Liam…err… thank you for your compliments," Sarah finally said, almost stuttering.

"How did you know my name? I can't remember telling you my name though," a puzzled Liam queried.

"Oh that erm err your name," Sarah stammered and was annoyed at herself for being unable to gather either herself or her words together.

"Yes, my name. How did you get to know my name?" Liam insisted, feigning seriousness.

"Your mother mentioned it today, a couple of minutes ago," Sarah finally blurted, letting out the first believable lie that came to her head. She hoped Liam found her answer satisfactory and let her be. She wanted him to be around so badly and now she couldn't stand herself in his presence. She was embarrassing herself and needed to get away from him.

"I need to use the restroom, ma'am," Sarah said loudly enough for Mrs. Jameson to hear.

"Oh sure you can, Liam kindly show her the way to the guest toilet," Mrs. Jameson said to her son.

Liam, who couldn't stop himself from looking at Sarah raised his hands towards a direction and led the way, Sarah followed, behind him. Liam's height was pretty obvious; he appeared to be a little too tall for his age. Sarah looked up to his back view during their journey to the toilet. She confessed to liking what she saw to herself.

"Oh my God this boy is actually hot, look at his shoulders and biceps. He seems very polite too and cute. I am such an idiot, why didn't I speak when he was talking to me? I hope he speaks to me again, I won't blow my chance this time. What if he tries to steal a kiss? Oops," Sarah thought, but quickly removed such a dirty thought from her mind.

Liam waited outside the guest toilet for Sarah to return. She was startled by his presence when she got out and met him standing there, waiting for her.

"Oh you waited" Sarah said in a shy way.

"Yes I did, I wasn't exactly sure that you could find your way back to the living room without my help," Liam said, trying to be as gentlemanly as possible.

"Nothing could have gone wrong you know, I could not have gotten lost or something," Sarah said chuckling.

"Okay you're right. If you cancel out the logic of my first reason for waiting for you then I will say the second."

"Oh there are two reasons, alright, go on let's hear the other reason," Sarah teased, she appeared to be comfortable with the conversation and was now leaning against the wall.

"The second reason is because I want to see your dress again. I told you you look beautiful in it the other time but you didn't say anything."

"Oh that, I apologize. Thanks."

"This is crimson red, right?" Liam asked, making it obvious that he wants the conversation to continue.

"Are you trying to flirt with me? You barely know me," Sarah responded.

"Well, that's not it and as regards to barely knowing you, I think that is about to change," Liam said smiling.

"What does that even mean?" Sarah asked, smiling sheepishly.

"You will find out later, let's go back before they come looking for us," Liam said, stepping aside to make room for Sarah to go ahead of him.

"Okay, I need to calm down and collect myself. Did Liam just flirt with me? What's that smile on his face? That was smooth though, Liam is cool. Way cooler than I thought and expected. Looks like today isn't bad after all," Sarah thought, smiling to herself while trying to hide her excitement.

The table was already set when both Liam and Sarah got down the stairs. Mr. Jameson waved to them to join in. At the table, a delicious meal awaited them. Both families had begun eating in silence. While eating, Liam whispered jokes to her which had her smiling throughout the meal. At the end of dinner, Liam volunteered that himself and Sarah would clear the table and also do the dishes. The rest of their families left them to it.

"Why would you volunteer my effort into something without informing me at first?" Sarah spoke first, breaking the awkward silence between them.

"I'm sorry if that made you angry, I thought you'd like to clean the table with me," Liam replied apologetically.

"With you? What do you mean by that?" Sarah queried raising her eyebrows for effect.

"Erm nothing," Liam said, almost stuttering. "It is just that I'll like to know you and become your friend if you'd let me," Liam said, struggling to finish his statement while putting on a very cute face.

"Oh okay there's no problem then, I am okay with that," Sarah assured him.

"So, hi I'm Liam," Liam said waving his hands and smiling.

"I know that's your name silly, I'm Sarah," Sarah said before letting out a loud and hearty laugh.

The duo got along well from that point and Sarah found out a couple of interesting things about Liam. It turned out that he was born a day before Sarah, and his favorite meal in the world was the blueberry oatmeal made by his mum and he wouldn't stop bragging about his mother's recipe. Sarah also discovered that she might not be an introvert after all. Especially when she's around him because she had been smiling ever since they had started talking and she had been letting him into her mind and head willingly.

When they were done doing the dishes, they joined the rest of their family in the garden. The garden was also a reflection of the interior of the Jameson's house. From the look of it, one can clearly see that it is properly catered for. The garden was properly mowed and the flowers and vegetables were properly tendered.

Mr. Jameson was something when Liam and Sarah got to the garden. He was talking about his past work experiences and their old residential area. He confessed to being scared of the fact that the apartment is haunted because something important to him is always missing every morning. His wife, Mrs. Jameson corroborated most of his stories and they both laughed out loud.

Marcus and his wife also shared a few stories. Mostly, the famous and embarrassing ones. For instance, they told the story of when Sarah had at a very young age wanted to be a beauty queen so bad she wore her mother's jewelry and fashion accessories. She got into trouble one day, when she wore her mother's red lipstick and it made a mess on her face, to the point where she got scared by seeing herself in the mirror and ran to her mother. At the end of the story, all eyes were on Sarah but she didn't feel embarrassed.

After a while, Marcus announced that he and his family would be taking their leave soon. Mr. Jameson feigned an unhappy face which made everyone burst out laughing again. He pleaded with Marcus to stay some more, at least for some wine and Marcus agreed. Mr. Jameson instructed Liam to get him a wine from the cellar.

He stood up to go and asked if Sarah could come with him because he will need a hand in putting some of the wines down, then back in place. Liam gestured to Sarah to come with him and she took her time before doing that. She sat for a while looking at her parents, especially her father, waiting for him to object but for some reason he didn't, so she left with Liam.

" I am not sure but it seems to me that you didn't want to come with me to the cellar, I'm very sorry for disturbing you and crossing boundaries," Liam apologized.

"No, actually that is not it. I don't set boundaries for my friends, even though I don't have many. The reason why I didn't get up to follow you immediately was because of my father," Sarah said, with her face grimaced.

"Oh what about him?" Liam asked in a rather calm way, lowering his voice and almost whispering as if Sarah's father was behind him.

"It's a long story Liam, the story of my life," Sarah replied with disappointment and helplessness buried deep in her voice.

"I thought friends didn't keep secrets from each other," Liam said with a smile on a bid to ease the ongoing tension.

"Well..." Sarah stutters at first.

"It's nothing serious, just that he can be so domineering and commanding. Imagine, I don't even have the right to wear the clothes I'd like to wear. He always wants his will to triumph, which doesn't make me happy. I really loved the dress I was going to wear instead of this. I looked more beautiful wearing that."

"You look beautiful in this too," Liam interjected. Sarah then apologized instantly.

"But I honestly think you should try to be more expressive about the things you want so that it can be clear and heard. You father is like that because of who he is, but he's getting away with it because of the way you are. You don't look like you can toughen up or stand your ground when there's a need."

"You know he's my father, right? And I can't just talk to him as I please or want," Sarah said, reminding Liam of what he seems to be forgetting. "I know he is your father and I know you have to respect and not fear him, there's a difference between those two."

"Oh okay, I will try. Now, what do you mean that I can't toughen up when need be?" Sarah said after folding her arms.

"What I am saying is; you look so fragile and you must be," Liam said.

"No, I'm not fragile. Maybe I look like I am but I'm not fragile. What do you mean? Do I look like an egg?" Sarah smiled.

"That's not how I mean it and you know it," Liam smiled.

"I am not fragile, I'm strong so strong and hard," Sarah said trying to convince herself.

"Show me what you can do then," Liam dared Sarah.

On hearing this Sarah gave Liam a punch on his shoulders which had little effect on him and giggled. When she attempted to do it again, Liam grabbed her hand suddenly and pulled her closer to himself. An awkward silence spread across the whole room and the duo stood still looking at each other for a long time. Sarah finally removed herself from the entanglement and looked away.

Liam was embarrassed and he tried to apologize, but Sarah insisted that she was not pissed. Liam picked the wine and led the way out of the wine cellar. Back in the garden, the families enjoyed the wine. Even though it had a little alcohol in it Mr. Jameson insisted on everyone having a share.

Shortly after, when it was almost evening, Marcus announced on behalf of his family their intention to leave.

"I think we will have to head home now. Thank you very much for hosting us, we hope to be able to repay the favor soon," Marcus said, standing up with glass of wine in his hand. Some pleasantries were exchanged between the families and goodbyes were said. All the while, Sarah and Liam avoided each other. Liam felt ashamed of himself and Sarah on the other hand felt as though she had overreacted or could have handled the situation better.

At home, Marcus did the unexpected. He expressed his displeasure with the Jamesons. He told his wife that he didn't like them and would appreciate if the bond they are trying to build with them was severed. His wife asked profusely what went wrong as she honestly thinks they are very nice people and they were received in the best way possible. Marcus insisted and hammered on the fact that he knows best and his opinion must hold. Sarah heard him saying this and her heart broke even more. She went into her room and shut the door, her mind flashed back to the day and how it was so unbelievably great until the later part. She remembered what happened in the wine cellar with Liam.

"I wonder what he was trying to do. Kiss me? What does he take me for or think of me? We barely even know each other, but...but I somehow wish he had done it though, I wonder what it feels like to be kissed. I wonder how good it would feel to be wrapped in his arms. Liam is a really sweet boy, I enjoyed his company. I really hope to see him again and we become friends. He's even more lovable than I expected him to be."

Sarah's thought process was rudely interrupted by her siblings. They came inside to talk about the Jameson's and how they had enjoyed the day. When Joan left, Joan started a conversation about Liam. She teased her sister about how cool she thinks he is and asked what happened during the time that they were alone together. Sarah wasn't going to tell them any of it except the fact that he was a nice boy indeed and she enjoyed her time with him.

"Are you sure that's all there is to know, because I saw the way he could not get his eyes off you. It was almost like you should live with him forever," Joan said smiling.

"I have no idea what you are talking about though, we just became friends that's all and we spoke about very random things," Sarah said, trying to hide her smile.

"Okay then, if you say so but I honestly up you two will get closer and know each other better. You look good together," Joan said before leaving the room.

"Thanks," Sarah replied as ordinarily as possible. "Please remember to shut my door."

Alone in her room, she thinks some more about Liam before falling into a deep sleep.

The next few days came and she noticed that she hadn't seen Liam or heard his parents calling out for him. She discarded this thought at first and decided to pay it no attention. After a few more days, she got bothered and decided to take a bold step and go and ask after her new friend at his house.

So on one quiet morning, Sarah waited for everyone in her house to take their leave and she stepped out. She wore one of her best dresses for obvious reasons; in hopes to see Liam. When she got to the Jameson's house she knocked gently on the door and waited for a response. When she didn't get any she turned around to leave disappointed and annoyed. Just when she was about to be out of sight from the Jameson's house she heard someone calling out to her, she looked back and it was Mrs. Jameson. Sarah went closer to her.

"Good day ma'am, how are you?" Sarah said.

"Hey hello beautiful, I apologize for not answering on time, I was away far gone into the chores I was doing in the house," Mrs. Jameson said with a broad smile plastered on her face and a handkerchief on her hand. She truly looked like she had been busy.

"Oh that's fine, ma'am," Sarah said letting the annoyance she had been feeling previously disappear.

"So, can I ask why you are here?" Mrs. Jameson inquired.

"oh ma'am, I came to check on Liam. To see if he is well and maybe around," Sarah said in the most friendly and casual way possible.

"That's so nice of you, although Liam no longer stays here. It's a quite complicated matter but he

no longer stays here and won't be coming back,"
Mrs. Jameson said with a sad face.

Sarah didn't understand what she said fully, but
seeing Mrs. Jameson's face she knew not to ask
any more questions.

"Alright ma'am, good bye ma'am," Sarah said and
turned to go back. She had only taken a few steps
before tears started flowing from her eyes. She
wondered why she was crying and she gave herself
an answer. She had fallen in love with Liam even
though they barely know each other. She hated
herself for doing this and she got mad at Liam, at
herself and everything. That night she cried herself
to sleep and thought about Liam for several more
days. It was sad.

# Chapter Three

A number of years passed, and Sarah and her family changed their area of residence, the Jamesons did the same and Sarah lost contact with Liam. They never met or spoke again, and life went on. Something very significant happened in Sarah's life after she went to college. Her father, Marcus got himself in some trouble with a crime lord. It involved borrowing a huge amount of money.

Gustavo was the most dreaded man in the entire city. He ran a casino to cover up his crime schemes, but everyone knew not to have anything to do with him. Unfortunately for Marcus, his friends introduced him to a reckless life of gambling in casinos. On his first night, he was totally unaware of the tricks of the game and this made it possible for him to get duped easily.

He lost so much more, and he had to borrow more at a breakneck interest rate from Gustavo. Gustavo lent him the money gladly, with the evil intent of trapping him more. In one night, Marcus lost more money than he had made in his entire life.

A few weeks later Gustavo came asking for his money with his scary looking boys. Marcus was having a discussion with him when Sarah walked in. On seeing Sarah, he spoke to Marcus about a deal which involved Sarah getting married to him in exchange for the borrowed sum. Marcus asked for some time to think about it. While he was thinking Gustavo employed every form of threat and pressure, he knew to get him to succumb and he finally did.

So, on one cool evening, Marcus called his daughter in to have a discussion with her. He spent a long time talking about how much he had sacrificed for her and the rest of their family and how he had always looked out for them, especially Sarah and he now expects her to do the same. He made Sarah assure him she would do whatever he asked of her. When he finally informed her of his plans to get her married to Gustavo the crime lord,

Sarah almost broke down in shock. She couldn't believe her ears and it was as though she was dreaming. She hated that man so much even without knowing or meeting with him.

She thought so much about what her father had said for several days. She spoke endlessly with her mom about it but as usual, she was helpless. Sarah eventually gave in seeing how serious Gustavo had become about harming her father. Although, she cried every day and wished for a miracle to make things turn around for her sake.

The wedding was planned and as the day drew near, Sarah got consumed in sadness and fear and she stopped speaking to everyone. She didn't feel excited to do anything. On the night before, Joan came into her room to talk to her. Sarah heard a slight knock on the door and asked the person to come in.

"It's me," Joan said in a hushed tone.

"Oh Joan, I'm really not in the mood to talk now and I'm sleepy."

"I know, and I understand, I only came to tell you that I understand your pain and I also hate how you are always made to do the things you actually don't want to do. I'd like to inform you that I look up to you for strength and I will always root for you in every situation," Joan said before turning back to leave.

Sarah got up and hugged her as tight as possible, and they both broke down in tears. When Joan left, Sarah thought about the things she had said, and she drew strength from it. She chose to abandon the forced wedding and run away from home. She didn't know what the future held, but she was not willing to get married to Gustavo and she never would. She took some of her valuable possessions and left without looking back. She went to begin a new life in another city.

# Chapter Four

Sarah got out of the yellow taxi and threw her muffler around her neck. It was overused and over-worn but still kept its lustre. It was her go-to accessory whenever she was uncertain of what to wear. She was just three months into her job as a Radiologist at the Saint James State Hospital. It had been all she had ever wanted even though she wasn't going to become a radiologist without her father's dictation, she's now determined to give her very best.

All her life, she had wanted to be a doctor but at age ten, she found out she was not good around blood, but her love for medical practice was vanishing and she was ready to settle for anything outside the entire field. But her father had entered the scene as usual and somehow made her go into college to study radiology instead, but nonetheless Sarah was still determined to be the best in her field.

"You say you can't work in a hospital if you faint at the sight of blood, that's okay. You can be a radiologist then and that works just as well," her father had said then. Her father had always chosen a lot of things for and Sarah hated this. Sarah had looked to her mother but her blonde model like mother said nothing to support her. She was alone but she never gave up.

She pushed her way through as a Radiologist embracing the strength of the human intellect and technology to locate problems in the human body and setting the doctor's work in motion. At that point, there was nothing more gratifying in her life and she knew she was good at it. Everyone at Saint James was talking about her.

However, for all her quick fame, she knew she wasn't taking home any award that night. She was still a newbie and most of the time; the award for the Employee of the Year often went to the doctors. The geeks in glasses, as the people at her end of the hospital referred to them.

Sarah kicked hard at the snow to make her way up the steps to the event. The thundering applause told her that she was really late. A few minutes and she would miss the speech by the recipient of the award. Who could it be? She wondered as she ran, pulling her coat tighter against her shivering skin as she made her way to the door. There was no one waiting to open the door for her, no one cared to for they were all focused on the man on the stage. It was her boss, everyone's boss.

Dr. Michael Wellington was a British man with the eyes of an Asian. One could never truly tell if his eyes were small or if they were only squinted because he smiled all the time.

"I feel happy about days like this," he started. "All year round, we work all day long and some of us, night shifts even so that we can save lives. Someone comes in with a broken arm, we take them in. Someone has a failing heart; we take them in because we have the brightest minds that the state of Michigan can offer." There was another round of applause as Sarah searched the tables for a vacant seat, there was none. So, she moved to the wall next to the janitors who were pleased to have her company.

Her eyes were fastened onto Dr. Michael's until she felt another stare on her. There was a man in one of the tables at the centre of the hall, wearing a tuxedo like many of the male doctors seated there. He was young, perhaps the youngest of the lot there and one that she had never come across before. It was hard to tell if he was a staff because she had not seen him in all her time at Saint James, but he was seated and wearing a tuxedo, so Sarah knew she had to be wrong.

What struck Sarah even more is the fact that he looked so much like Liam. She wished that it would be him so badly, but at the same time she suppressed the idea of going to ask him if he's the one. Suddenly, he got up and started walking towards her. Her heart skipped a beat and threatened to jump out from her mouth. She kept praying silently to herself.

"The awardee this year is a pure genius. I see much of myself in this person. I mean I walk down the hall and I find myself wondering who put a mirror in the hallway until I hear 'good morning Dr. Michael'. Then I realize that it's not me, it's another genius," the hearty Dr. Michael continued. Sarah laughed as did everyone in the hall. For a moment, she had taken her eyes off the strange man in the tuxedo before she felt a gentle pat on her shoulder.

"Take my seat. It's over there," he said with a voice so calm that Sarah felt warmth crawl up her skin. Seeing him earlier, she had not noticed his eyes until he was close to her. His hair was combed back neatly in curls and he had a rich politician smile.

*Who are you?* Sarah wanted to ask but as always, she said something different.

"I can't take your seat. It's yours," she told him.

"Well, I insist, please," he asked again, waving for her to move past him. Sarah wanted to argue but her words seemed caught up in her tongue. It was his disarming eyes, she realized. Eyes were not supposed to be so green. It was criminal.

Reluctantly, she agreed and made her way across the tables to where the gentleman had stood from. She took her seat and looked back at him, but his eyes were not on her anymore. Dr. Michael had everyone's attention again.

"So, a patient comes up to me in my office and goes like 'I think I am going to die'. That shocked me, I must admit, and I asked the man why he thought so. He gave the name of some doctor in some hospital that I will not mention." Dr. Michael dragged the last words knowing that everyone knew which hospital he spoke of as murmurs sprang across all tables before he continued.

"Then this other doctor in my office says 'why good sir, let me take a quick look at you. You seem like a healthy man to me'. Those should have been my words, but I was still in shock. I followed them both to the lab and the doctor ran tests. Alas! We were going to have a surgery. 'I will handle it, no problem', the doctor said, and I backed away.

This doctor was on a roll that I did not want to stop, plus, I wasn't feeling too surgical that week. Two days later, we had a surgery and-" Dr. Michael leaned towards the microphone as he spoke and stared at his captivated audience. It was a pause that made everyone seated quite hungry. He had given away the fact that the awardee of the night was a doctor, but not much else. Taken by the confidence in the doctor's tone, he had to have been male.

"Well, let me call him out to finish the tale. People, please hop to your feet and let's give a rewarding welcome to Liam McCauley," he announced.

Sarah looked about the tables around her searching for Liam McCauley. His was a name that she had heard quite a lot around the hospital, but she had never seen his face. He is handsome; was the rumour out of the nurses' quarters. The doctors thought him smart and reserved. They thought the name akin to arrogance in Sarah's end of the hospital. All had summed up the image of a tall handsome doctor with a high chin of arrogance about him, but no one matching that description got up around her.

She was astonished when she saw the young man with the captivating green eyes pick up his pair of glasses from the table she was seated at before he headed towards the podium. The applause grew louder as he walked up to the stage and extended his hand to Dr. Michael. The hearty Brit pulled his younger counterpart into an embrace before stepping back.

The young handsome doctor came to the microphone and paused a moment as he scanned the room for the people who watched him.

"I hate his guts; he is so cocky and full of himself." Sarah heard from the woman seated next to her. It surprised her since that very woman had been sitting next to Liam not long before he had given up his seat. For reasons even Sarah could not put her finger to, she disliked the woman instantly.

"I know many of you do not share my beliefs. You think I am a little rigid. I am the geek in the classroom who sees only the ones and the zeroes. While that might be true, I see myself as a true believer in humanity, in knowledge and medicine. Dr. Wellington was being modest by saying I went through the surgery alone. I didn't. I had help from people who put their trust in me and in science, an unwavering belief that we could save the man's life, a man who had given up all hope. That man is alive today not because I am a genius, but because of everyone here who trusts one another," Liam said before he stepped back for Dr. Michael to come forward.

"Like I said, he is too modest. Please another round of applause for our Employee of the Year, Dr. Liam McCauley," Dr. Michael said, and the room was filled again with a symphony of clapped hands.

"I am sure Liam must have bit his tongue reciting that last part of the speech. Trust, my foot, he-" The woman next to Sarah continued.

"Excuse me," Sarah butted in before she could stop herself. It was her nature, her curse to never be able to turn a blind eye. The woman looked at her with kind eyes. It was obvious that her hatred was only for Liam McCauley.

"Why do you dislike him so much?" Sarah asked.

"You are new here, right?" The woman asked her as though it was the answer to all her curiosity. Sarah nodded her head. Longevity was a very big bargaining chip at the hospital. This, she had caught on to quickly. Despite her good work, she was still at the bottom of the food chain.

"He's back at the hospital now, so you'll find out soon enough and when you do-" the woman moved closer to Sarah to whisper "-don't let him see your red eyes, it makes him happy."

Sarah looked back to the podium at the calm and sweet looking man who stood next to Dr. Michael for a photograph. She could see nothing more than his aura of intelligence and pretty boy looks. He was the man who had offered her his seat just a few minutes before. The woman's words seemed preposterous to her.

Liam always seemed to be at an arm's length from her throughout the rest of the program as she grew more curious about him and wanted to speak to him. Why did the staffs dislike him so much? It made no sense to her.

Eventually, when the program was over, she fought her way through the crowd of people to get to Liam as he headed out first. There was a Lamborghini waiting for him outside with a driver she could not see through the tinted glass.

"Dr. McCauley, Dr. McCauley," she called him before he heard her. She had expected a smile from him but there was none. It seemed as though he was angry about her delay and wanted to be done with her as soon as he could. In his left hand was his glass plague.

"Sorry, how may I help you?" He asked her sharply. The gentleman who had offered her his seat was gone.

"Eh- I wanted to thank you for earlier and congratulate you on your award. I was the lady who you gave your seat to," she spoke faster than she had planned but it was his intense stare that had her uneasy.

"Oh, it was you. Thank you," he said before turning away from her. Sarah was left standing there feeling unsatisfied. She wanted to tell him how he looked so much like someone she knew  from her teenage years and even had the same name as him. But Liam was not ready for that chat, he owed her nothing else, but his obvious disinterest troubled her.

The door to the driver's seat came open and a man who was a physical twin of Liam came out. The only difference between the two men was the ponytail the driver had and his casual 50 CENT t-shirt.

"Did we bag it?" Liam's twin brother asked him as he came towards the car. Liam tossed the plague at his brother who fumbled it in his hands a little before he had a firm grasp on it.

"I'd have killed you if it had broken," Liam said jovially as he pulled open his door.

"You did that thing where you walked from the door when they called you?" His brother asked him.

"You bet," Liam said as he got into the car. His brother took a long look at a stunned Sarah before he got into the car after Liam and the twins zoomed off.

Sarah was left outside feeling a seething rage build up within her. He had not been kind to her. She had just simply been a prop to him so that he could make a long walk towards the podium once he was called out. *What an ass!* She thought with disdain before she caught familiar faces wave at her. She walked to join them, feeling a new kinship with them. They all disliked Liam McCauley.

***

Sarah took off her muffler and lay on her bed thinking about the events that had happened that night. Through it all, only one face stuck in her mind; Liam McCauley and that was the face of the man that came into her head. She remembered Liam her from her past and wondered if he was the same person. But she was sure he wasn't rude as this new Dr. Liam and he couldn't have grown into that. She missed Liam as he was the only person she had ever loved. However, she doesn't care one bit about this Liam, she shoves off the idea that they might be the same person and decides to continue her dislike for Dr. Liam.

She slept that night with a smile on her face as she pictured a look of awe on Liam McCauley's perfect face as he watched her walk past him to win the next year's Employee of the Year award. Something about it turned her on more than she had intended it to.

It was  unknown to Sarah that within the space of time that she had lost contact with Liam, a lot had happened to him. First, he had discovered that the Jameson's were not his biological parents and that they were actually wealthy people who lived very far away and that he actually has a twin brother. Liam had also had an accident that made him lose most of his childhood memory, which was why he was unable to recall her face correctly.

Liam's new parents were not the exact model of the best parents either, and they paid little attention to shaping Liam and his twin brother into well-mannered gentlemen. All these things dealt a blow on Liam's character development and played a great role in who he is now- the cocky and arrogant Liam.

Liam McCauley sat in the Jacuzzi watching his twin brother play around with his girlfriends. There were three of them with names that seemed cut of a movie strip club scene; Ginger, Sugar and Baby. Connor McCauley played on the famed family heirloom, the McCauley piano as the ladies in their lingerie flocked around him dancing to music that could not have been what Connor was playing. They were all drunk.

Liam was never one to party even though his family was wealthy. The fact that he never had a childhood like that made him somewhat different. His great-great grandfather had made so much money in Ireland before moving to America and had still made even more of a fortune still in liquor. Connor was in charge of the family business while Liam had forfeited his seat on the company board for a career in medicine much to the displeasure of their late parents. He was the serious one in the family and his father's last wish had been that he stay close to Connor to be a good influence on him.

He sighed and was about to reach for a towel when he saw the most petit of Connor's girlfriends, Baby walk towards the Jacuzzi. That was his queue to leave, he knew. Baby pulled his towel out of his reach and put her hands on his shoulders to massage him.

"No, thank you," he told her. "I have to turn in early tonight." He brushed her hand away and she held onto his towel with a pity pout on her face.

"Connor, your brother is a *meanie*. He will not play with me," Baby called to Connor. Connor stopped playing the piano and looked to Liam for a moment. They were twins and though they did not share a telepathic link, they could read one another's faces. Connor for all his love for trouble knew when not to tease Liam.

"Give Liam his towel, Baby and come hang out with the fun McCauley. I'll let you play the piano," Connor said to Baby and she dropped the towel without much thought. Liam took the towel and wrapped it around himself before heading for his bedroom. He disliked having company in the house, but understood that Connor was not built as he was. His twin brother did not share his love for quiet.

The plague was on his shelf as were the other awards he had won growing up. Most were in sports as his father had wanted. The only two silver medals he had were in tennis, losing to Connor back in High School. He was a winner but that came at a price.

"Your clique goes a long way to determine who you become," his father used to say. "You see someone below you, you let them know. You never ever let them pull you back because that's all they do. You take their hands and they infect you with their low self-esteems and fears of the future. But you can't feel that because you are a McCauley," he heard his father's voice in his head as he looked at the plague.

"I won it, dad," Liam muttered under his breath as he fell into bed. He was exhausted. The night had gone fairly well, as much as he had expected it to. There had been no bumps, so he closed his eyes and let himself slip into the darkness behind his eyes where his peace lay awaiting him.

***

Morning always came like magic every day. Liam knew the mechanics behind sleeping and could teach on it for hours, but his only willful audience was Connor who would throw a tomato at him rather than listen to him blab about 'medical nonsense' as he called it. Liam put on his flip-flops and headed downstairs for breakfast. His first engagement for the day was a surgery at ten a.m. and that gave him a few hours to kill before heading to the hospital.

Coming down the stairs to the kitchen, Liam found Connor sitting alone on the counter with a bowl of cereal. Liam realized the other reason he liked Monday mornings. It was because all Connor's girlfriends would all be gone, leaving the house to him, his twin brother and best friend, and the maids. He sat down and made himself a bowl of cereal also.

"You've been sleeping a lot these days. I thought you'd been having one of your nights in the library," Connor said before pouring more milk into his bowl. The maid was late again, and both men were too lazy to whip up a meal.

"I have a surgery today. I always like to get enough sleep, so I don't end up losing focus while cutting through a living and breathing human," Liam replied. The loud sigh that Connor gave told him that he had just answered a rhetorical question. The science stuff always bored Connor.

"What about Stephanie?" Connor asked Liam about his ex. That was Liam's turn to sigh. He knew Connor for all his brilliance had problems remembering people, which meant that the only reason he would remember Liam's ex was if she had spoken to Connor recently.

"What about Stephanie?" Liam threw the question back at his brother. Connor raised his hands up in a gesture of peace before Liam would think to take his head.

"I am just worried about you. We are thirty-two and I think you need a woman in your life," Connor said putting aside his bowl.

"It is good advice surely since it is coming from you," Liam snickered.

"Yes, coming from me; it's total wisdom. I have three. How many do you have?" Connor asked him. They both burst into laughter at his failed attempt at a serious face. When they were both sober from their little laughter, Connor tried the serious countenance again.

"I worry about you. You just live with your large books and you are not alive, not really-" Connor raised his warning finger before Liam could speak against him "- and you don't have friends. I am all your friends and that is sad. More importantly, you don't have a woman."

"I don't need one yet," Liam replied with a mouth full of soaked cereal. He could not wait to put an end to the familiar argument.

"Stephanie-" Connor started before Liam cut him off.

"We were not on the same wavelength. She had no steel. She was not ambitious enough for me; had no fighting spirit. She liked everything I liked."

"That is not weird. Most men think that is lucky," Connor told him.

"No one is that compatible. I think she doesn't know what she wants, and I can't be with a woman like that; period!" Liam got up on his feet. "Now, if you will excuse me..."

"What about the lady by the hospital on Saturday?" Who? That was the question Liam asked instantly. He didn't know the lady his brother spoke of.

"The cute one with the muffler and coat talking to you when I came to pick you up," Connor tried again, but Liam could not remember the lady. He knew he had spoken to someone, but he had been in a hurry to get away from the crowd that he had barely taken any notice of her. He peeled at his brain but remembered nothing.

"I don't remember," he replied finally. He put his empty bowl in the sink and headed for the stairs.

"She was cute, just saying and she seemed to be into you. I mean how many people at the hospital even speak to you?" Connor shrugged, Liam looked at the time and realized that he could not indulge his brother any further. He hurried up the stairs for a shower.

***

The Saint James' hospital was the largest in the city and the perfect place for Liam. The moment he had decided on studying medicine, he had also decided on working there as their youngest surgeon before his record was broken quite recently by someone getting in at age twenty-eight after a small stint elsewhere, he was finally home. He parked his father's old Mercedes in the parking lot and headed in for work. He had about an hour to prep for surgery. It was one of the ones that he loved, the ones which had audiences from the College.

He took a good look at himself in the mirror before he got out of his car. Liam had never been particular about his looks, but he knew he was just as handsome as Connor was. In college, girls had tried to get either of the brothers but now, he had no interest in that. When he was probably thirty-four or five and with the office of the Chief Surgeon, he would consider marriage.

The nurses nodded to him as he walked into the hospital and headed for the elevator. One of them rushed after him with a notepad, bumping into him as he stopped suddenly in front of the playground. It was the large space that had been transformed just days before into the hall where he had been awarded the best employee in the five storey building. With a satisfied smile, he continued on his way to the elevator and the nurse followed after him.

"Dr. McCauley, you have a surgery in an hour. It's eh-" She jumped into the elevator after him "-a man with an inoperative bullet in his brain. It hasn't killed him yet but it's only a matter of time," she stammered on before she met Liam's cold stare.

"I am sorry. I was instructed by Dr. Wellington to run through the details of the surgery with you again," she apologized.

"How many colleagues are here?" He asked her.

"Three accompanied by four professors," she said. That was all Liam wanted to know. The nurse knew to stop when he nodded and looked up at the elevator screen. They were almost on the third floor.

"Thank you," Liam said before heading out of the elevator. Something about his words seemed to have caught the nurse off guard and she froze.

Liam could not tell what it was that had made her react so strangely, but he discarded it as soon as he was in the hallway and almost at his office. He walked past the theatre and looked inside at the blue curtains with a smile on his face. That was his stage.

Getting to his office, he took off his jacket and changed into a freer and more suitable outfit for the operation. It was going to be an easy one, a surgery that only relied on his meticulous skill set. He made his way into the bathroom and washed his face before heading for the theatre. Slapping his face, he killed the smile on his face before he made his way into the theatre.

He nodded to the men that were going to assist him that morning. Their faces were hidden behind their face masks, but he knew their eyes. They were his superiors, which made it all the better for him. He looked up at the large screen that overlooked the theatre. There were five aristocratic looking men, including Dr. Michael Wellington who was in an oversized suit like the other men. The students were seated also, stretching their necks even before the operation had started.

Liam bowed to them all like the performer that he was before he put on his gloves and pulled his face mask over his mouth and nose. The man with the bullet in his head was mid-fifties and seemed oddly satisfied to be in the theatre also.

"What is your name?" Liam asked the man as he always asked his patients for trophy piling.

"Benjamin," the man answered.

"Is this your first time having a surgery?" Liam asked the man as the nurse held the anaesthetic tube at the ready. Benjamin nodded with a smile on his face.

"Just relax. Everything will go perfectly," Liam assured the man on the bed.

"I know. Just make me look good in front of the young ones, yeah?" Benjamin asked with a humour that Liam was unfamiliar with. Liam stepped back and watched the man as his nose was covered and the gas given to him. He had never seen anyone so happy to undergo a surgery. He was used to being the most confident one in the room and that startled him for a moment until the man was out cold.

"Good luck, surgeons," Dr. Wellington's voice droned through the speakers and Liam opened his hand to be handed the scalpel. The skin tissue would be first, then a hole in the skull and then he would reach in for the bullet. *Easy peasy*, Liam thought as he began under the watchful eyes of his eager audience.

Thirty minutes passed and Liam dropped the bullet onto the tray. He stepped back to allow another surgeon to continue. There was a round of applause that was quickly quieted by one of the professors as the operation was still going on. Liam removed his apron and put down the scalpel. Standing by the side of the bed, he nodded to Dr. Wellington and to his audience who were all in awe at his meticulous performance. Everyone had a childish glint in their eyes except for the woman at the back who looked unimpressed.

*Who are you and why do you look familiar?* Liam wondered. It unsettled him greatly that there was someone who did not think his work was special and even looked like someone he knew but can't remember.

# Chapter Five

Sarah had not thought about Liam's behaviour throughout the weekend until Monday had come and the idea of seeing Liam's face. However, it did not vex her so much this time. It made her smile as she envisaged the sad look that would cross his face when she bested him. He was now her enemy and didn't even know it.

She had enough to buy a car, but she enjoyed the rigours of public transport; the noise, the view of the city in the early hours of the morning and being around people. There was something about watching people; the old and the young that excited her. They were so alive, full of strength and ambition, and that was her work; to put more people out on the streets with hope, strength, and ambition. Everyone deserves a healthy lifestyle she believed and she loved contributing her quota by helping to locate their medical issues.

Getting to the hospital early, she went to say hello to her favourite patients.

"You look more beautiful than you did on Friday. I don't get it. I don't understand it," Usman said the moment he saw Sarah walk into the ward. He had been in an accident and was paralysed from the neck down. It was required that x-rays be conducted on his body from time to time because of the severity  of the injury. Though Sarah felt he would have been focused on the pains he's experiencing, but Usman had been swelling. He had proposed to Sarah the moment he had gotten control of his hands back, but she had politely declined. Still, he flirted endlessly with her.

Usman used to be a small time novelist before his accident, and he appreciated Sarah's company much more because she seemed to be the only one to still have interests in fictional works. So, whenever she was free or running check-ups on him, she sat and listened to him craft new stories that he swore he was going to put in print once he could walk again.

"I am not marrying you, Usman. You should stop trying," Sarah told him with a smile as she tapped his foot with her pen. He shook his head. He could feel nothing. The same way she hasn't felt anything for any man since she was a teen when she had met Liam. It is easy to say he was the love of her life but how can he be that when she barely knew him. Again, if this person is the same Liam, she once loved then she doesn't want to have anything to do with him. For Sarah, no matter how good and handsome you might be, if you are as cocky as Dr. Liam then it's a no, no for her.

"No muffler today?" Usman asked her as she came to his side. Sarah touched her neck, forgetting that she had not used the muffler that day. It was unusual but she had woken up with clarity that day that had also transferred to her outfit decision making. She had gone for a pair of jeans and a sleeveless blouse.

"I guess so, Usman. Well, I need to go change and check on the others too," she told him.

"I'll write a bestseller and then I can pay for you to check on only me all day. How about that, Sarah?" He asked her. Sarah simply smiled and moved on to check on the others before she made her way to her office. The hospital did not have very many radiologists,   but Sarah never complained. She enjoyed her job and the less staffs there, the more people she got to help. She changed to her white pants and blouse; the hospital uniform, before heading out again.

On her way to the waiting room to get a cup of water, she met Dr. Wellington.

"Ah! The woman I have been looking for my whole life. Come, come Miss. Meyer," he bellowed to her. "Can I call you Sarah?" He asked her. Sarah had no problem with formalities or the lack of them, so she nodded her agreement.

"I want you to come to my office. There is something I want to discuss with you but-" He rubbed his right fingers together in indecisive thought before he spoke again "-you know what, follow me. We'll go to the theatre together and then go to my office afterwards. There is someone we need to pick up there," he told her, and Sarah knew her morning had already been decided.

Sarah had been excited to be summoned by Dr. Wellington but the timid smile on her face had faded when she had seen the surgeon pull down his face mask. Liam McCauley, she had almost spat the name out when she had seen his arrogant face. A little satisfaction had eased into her when she had seen his usually handsome face distort in confusion as their eyes met.

*Not everyone thinks you are special,* she thought with a wicked smile before she had exited the viewing room with Dr. Wellington.

Her professional face was back when she entered Dr. Wellington's office. It was the largest in the building but still felt like the smallest still because it was stocked with too many books. It made Dr. Wellington look like a librarian in a fantasy movie, with walls of books everywhere. The only thing that personified his office was the picture of his family on his desk.

"So, Sarah, we have a new patient and I feel a little biased in this case. The young man in question here is the son of my best friend from High School. He was unlucky to have been involved in an accident and it seemed like he might not be able to walk again. His father is devastated because this young man is great at football; the rugby sport with the helmet, you know that, I need you to carefully conduct a radioscopy on the young lad, it's a quite complicated medical condition that needs your attention, you can do this right?" Dr. Wellington asked Sarah and she nodded with a smile.

The Chief Doctor was a very kind man, everyone could tell at first glance. He was respected by all and thus, everyone jumped at the chance to impress him. At that very moment in his office, Sarah felt nothing more than the urge to prove herself to him, especially given the personal nature of the problem.

"I promise to do all within my power. Can I get to see the patient now?" Sarah asked, ready to work.

"We have to wait for one more person; the one who will work hand-in-hand with you," Dr. Wellington said as they both heard a knock on the door.

"Come in," Dr. Wellington shouted to the door and it came open. Sarah's face paled when she saw Liam McCauley walk towards her.

***

She straightened in her seat, keeping her eyes on the Chief Doctor alone. She did not want to look at Liam. It was bad enough that he was so close to her, but she could also smell his cologne. *Why is he here?* She asked herself the question but knew it was as rhetorical a question as any could get. Everyone knew Liam was the Doctor's favourite and the 'alleged' brightest also. Dr. Wellington would want only the best.

It did nothing to pacify her that he had ranked her alongside Liam. She wanted only to surpass him. She was already the youngest Radiologist but that was not enough to fluster Liam as he considered himself ahead of her.

"Do you two know one another?" Dr. Wellington asked the both of them.

"No," Sarah answered as she could feel Liam's probing stare on the side of her face, and it made her uneasy.

"No," he also answered before letting up on her face.

"Well, I leave it to the both of you to do the introductions," Dr. Wellington said nonchalantly. He reached into his drawer and pulled out a large folder. He pulled out two scans and handed one apiece to Sarah and Liam. Sitting back, he watched their faces hoping for good news.

"So, what do you think?" He asked them.

"This is-" Liam started, but Sarah spoke also at the same time. "No, you go first," Liam said to her.

"No, you can," Sarah told him wilfully.

"I insist, go ahead," Liam said before sinking into his seat. Sarah played back his words in her head hoping to find anything condescending about it but there was none. It was unusual that he would allow her to speak first given the kind of impression that he had left with her after the first night they had met. But she spoke. There was no point to keeping the boss waiting.

"These scans look quite difficult, but I am of the belief that it is not enough proof to write off the patient's chances. I also have to speak to the patient before I can give a verdict and conduct new ones," Sarah said. She looked to Liam after he had spoken but there was still nothing to read off his face.

"What about you, Liam?" Dr. Wellington asked him.

"As she said, this is not enough for us to come to a conclusion," Liam answered without much effort and enthusiasm.

"Well, Ash could be brought in in about twenty minutes, so please be ready to evaluate him. The scans were sent from another hospital, so I need you, Sarah to take new ones and assist Liam in taking new scans with our own equipment. Thank you both," Dr. Wellington said as he rose to his feet. Sarah and Liam also followed suit and headed out of the office.

Sarah opened the door and let herself out while Liam hurriedly caught the door before she could shut it behind her. In the hallway, he hurried after her, trying to catch up to her.

"Why do you dislike me?" He asked her when he came to her side. Sarah gave him no answer.

"Hey, hey, I saw you at the theatre. I thought that was just coincidence and then at the office- You don't like me very much and you are doing a terrible job at hiding that," he told her, coming to her fore. Sarah looked up at him with her meanest face, but he did not seem fazed by it. He only smiled down at her, expecting an answer from her.

"For a so called genius, you are quite forgetful," she snapped at him, crossing her arms across her chest.

Liam looked up at the ceiling and clasped his hands together as though in prayer as he thought. Where could he have met her? He wondered. There were too many staffs at the hospital and he only knew the faces that he came across every day. Having been away from the hospital for a while, he did not remember her face, so he did a guess.

"The award night," he asked her.

"Oh, so you remember. Wow! I take my words back. You are a genius," Sarah clamoured with unhidden sarcasm. She waited for an apology, but none came from him, so she brushed past him and continued towards the elevator.

"The boy will never walk again. I don't know why you gave the Chief hope. Do you want a promotion that bad?" Sarah stopped when she heard his words. Her eyes were red with anger as she turned back to face him.

"I did not offer any false hope and you- You agreed with me in there. Why did you do that if you didn't believe he would be able to walk?" Sarah asked him. Smitten with anger, she found herself walking back towards him with clenched fists. Up close, she looked intently at Liam and kept quiet for a while as he looked so much like Liam from her past now.

"Wait, are you sure you don't know me from anywhere else? I mean aside from the award night," Sarah asked, putting a serious face on.

"No, why are you asking?" Liam replied with a grimaced face.

"Nothing, you just look so much like someone from my past," Sarah said collecting herself together.

""It's definitely not me Sarah, I could not have met a person like you. That's not even possible," Liam said laughing.

"You know what? I hate you," Sarah said as she released her fist. She turned around and continued faster to the elevator. She was not going to allow him to taunt her anymore.

"I don't particularly like you either. Call that fair?" He shouted after her.

"I don't want to see you anywhere near the patient, keep your pessimistic and lying distance from him, I'll ask to work with another more positive doctor " Sarah shouted back as she made her way into the elevator.

Liam said something back, but she was glad that she heard none of it as the doors of the elevator closed. She rested easy against the wall of the elevator as she felt it descend. It annoyed her how easily he could crawl under her skin without even doing much. Taking deep breaths, she steadied herself and came to the waiting room. Soon enough, she knew that Ash would be wheeled into the hospital. Looking around, she was satisfied to find that Liam was nowhere in sight.

***

Ash was as downcast as most of the other patients who had come her way. He looked at everything about him with disinterest as he was wheeled to a bed in his new room. Usually, most of Sarah's patients were taken to the wards on the ground floor, but Ash was special. He was taken to one of the single rooms as he needed to be monitored.

"Hey there Ash, I am Sarah Meyer, but you can call me Sarah," Sarah introduced herself to him when they were finally alone. His eyes studied Sarah for a moment with interest before it suddenly left his eyes and he turned his head away from her.

"I want to sleep," he said firmly.

"You-" Sarah's words were cut short when she heard the door open behind her. Liam walked into the room.

"What are you doing here?" She asked him. He ignored her and walked past her to the side of the bed.

"We were tasked with him, were we not?" Liam said without looking at her. His studious eyes looked over the new patient for the comical feel. Ash's downcast countenance reaffirmed all that he had already believed. The man was without hope. Liam walked back to Sarah who was still glaring at him.

"The percentage of his recovery is in the zero points region and that is even for a percentage," he whispered to her.

"If you cannot wait for the x-ray results and you choose to say negative things then you may take your leave" Sarah said to him. Liam snickered and looked at her face hoping to see a waver in her words, but she showed none.

"Fine, fine, I don't want to be a part of this," he said in his hushed tone before walking out of the room. Sarah felt warmth spread across her breasts as she heard the sound of the door.

"Why are you smiling?" Ash asked her when he caught her smiling.

"Well, I have conquered the first hurdle in your recovery. The next one I have to overcome is you, Ash," she told him as she came towards his bed. This time, he did not look away from her. Something about her struck him this time around and captivated his attention. So, he kept his weary eyes open and listened to her.

# Chapter Six

ood *riddance*, Liam thought as he walked out of the room. He tried hard to make his ego accept the lie that he told it, but it was difficult for a man like him who was used to being respected by everyone he ever came across. His chest felt sour as he made his way towards the elevator. He cursed under his breath as he got inside the elevator as he waited for the doors to close, but a hand stopped it and a bed was wheeled in by two nurses.

"Dr. McCauley," one of the nurses dared to greet him and he nodded back to her. He kept his eyes on the screen of the elevator before he suddenly realized that he would not remember her face some other day just like with Sarah. So, he looked back at her and forced a smile so that it would not be awkward. She smiled back at him. She was a pretty woman, but Liam found himself comparing her with Sarah.

The nurse was about the same height as Sarah but wasn't as curvy as Sarah. Her face though pretty was round while Sarah's was model chiselled with cheek bones and a small mouth with wicked slim lips. Sarah's eyes though fiery were a tender blue, which was the reason that he found it easy to laugh in her face whenever she was angry but now, he was the one feeling terrible. Realizing that he had been staring too long, he turned away and walked out of the elevator once the doors opened.

He was halfway to his office when he realized that the thing, he really needed was a cup of coffee. He turned back to the elevator which was still in use. Too anxious to wait, he took the stairs down to the cafeteria.

Liam hardly ever sat at the cafeteria for lunch, but he decided to stay that day since there weren't many people around. Every other table was coupled or had groups of people sitting there, but he never minded the isolation. It gave him time to think.

*Why did you go to the room?* He asked himself. He was fuming over Sarah kicking him out of the room. She had warned him not to come and he had done so anyway. Liam wasn't used to taking orders from people he believed below his level, but that had not been the reason that he had defied her. Standing with her in the hallway after they had left Dr. Wellington's office, he had realized for the first time how beautiful she was.

"Curse you, Connor," he muttered into his cup before taking another sip. At the moment that she had confirmed that she had been the one that he had spoken to that night after the Awards Ceremony, Connor's comments about her had come back to plague his mind.

"She was cute, just saying and she seemed to be into you..." His twin brother had said earlier that morning. Connor apparently had only been right about the cute part. Sarah was certainly not into him, and for some reason, that didn't settle well with him. He had not been able to stop himself from looking at her as she had walked away from him, swaying her round hips in her feat of rage. Liam was not a lustful man, not like his brother Connor was and while he had chastised his brother for that many times, he had found himself a victim.

When she had turned around to face him, he had seen her face as though for the first time, her small mouth, and soft blue eyes. *But she kicked you out,* Liam's ego reminded him. So, he embraced his rage to escape the conflicting thoughts that had ravaged his mind since he had encountered Sarah Meyer.

***

Getting home, Liam had been ready to pour out his frustration on any of Connor's girls if they dared tease him that night, but Connor was home alone. Instead of heading up straight to his room, Liam took off his jacket, unbuttoned his shirt and sat next to Connor in the balcony overlooking the swimming pool.

"How was the surgery?" Connor asked and Liam looked at him with a mean look, forcing Connor to laugh. "You know I was teasing you. You are Liam McCauley, the best surgeon in Michigan and soon the best in America."

Liam smiled and looked at the lights playing alongside the ripples in the pool just like his brother had been before he had arrived.

"You had a sad vibe about you when you were coming towards me, so I had to try to lighten you up at least lest you infected me also. How was work?" Connor asked him. Liam sighed and sank back in the hand-woven seat.

"I met the girl you spoke about the night of the award," Liam started for the milder part of the story.

"Oh, oh, she was cute, wasn't she?" Connor asked him and Liam could not help the smile that crossed his face.

"But she pissed me off. There was this kid brought in today and Wellington asked us if the boy could walk again. I knew the boy had one in a million chances of walking again, but she just jumped in front of me and said that he might be able to. That is messed up. You were right that she was cute, I give you that but besides that, nah, she is too dreamy," Liam told his brother.

"Wow! Someone that doesn't agree with everything that Liam McCauley thinks; what a world, right," Connor humoured him. Liam had nodded before he realized that Connor was making a reference to Stephanie his ex. He made a swing for Connor's head but missed.

"Does she look like a mere hothead? It is a big thing to say a man can walk when he can't. So, do you think she is just a hothead?" Connor asked Liam. Liam fell silent for a moment as he contemplated his brother's question. Sarah had a temper, towards him but she was no hothead.

"I have to go upstairs," Liam told Connor. Going-upstairs was code for going to study.

"Dinner is ready if you want some," Connor reminded him before he entered the house.

"Have the maid send it to my room," Liam told his brother as he readied himself for a long night. For the first time in a long time, he felt that there was something he didn't know and someone else knew.

*Sarah, why do you think he can walk?* He asked himself as he picked out three books from his shelf and sat to read.

***

Liam woke up the next morning on his desk none-the-wiser than he had been the night before. There was a defined line between conventional medicine (him) and the alternative medicine (Sarah). He had slept with a question and had woken up with the same question. *Sarah, why do you think he can walk?*

Liam skipped breakfast that morning before heading to work. The nurses at the reception seemed to go pale as he made his way towards them that morning. He had never walked towards the counter in all his years at the hospital to speak to them. He always just headed for the elevator.

"Good morning, ladies," he said as he came to the counter. He was greeted by three big grins.

"Please, where is the office of a Sarah Meyer?" He asked them and they answered him promptly. "Thank you," he told them before heading away. Looking back at them, he realized that they were frozen also in awe. What had he said? He wondered as he came to Sarah's office. She was not in, so he told one of her colleagues to call his office when Sarah got in.

Liam sat in his office, took off his jacket and rolled up sleeves before washing his face. He wondered what would Connor would do in that kind of situation. His brother would kiss someone's foot just for the sake of his need. His needs were mostly unnecessary, but Liam saw no other prize greater than knowledge.

He took a deep breath when he got a call to his office. Sarah was around. He checked himself in the mirror one more time before heading for the elevator. He met Sarah on her way out of her office. She looked as lovely even though he expected her to be mean towards him. She had on a long loose blouse atop a grey pair of skin-tight jeans. Her thighs looked round in them, but he took his eyes off them as quickly as his mind had strayed.

"What can I do for you, Dr. McCauley?" She asked him nonchalantly as she continued walking. Liam followed after her, sighing in apology to his ego before he spoke.

"I think we got off on the wrong foot," he started, and Sarah halted unsure of what she had just heard. She turned around to face him. Her blue eyes scrutinized his as though searching for any con.

"Oh, really now," she spoke finally, folding her arms across her chest. Liam was quickly coming to understand that gesture for what it meant.

"I am a man of medicine as are you, a woman of medicine. I see possibilities and impossibilities. While I try to break the impossibilities, there are just some things that I don't even try. So, I ask this question with no pun intended. Why do you think he can walk?" Liam asked her. Sarah smiled at him. Liam counted the seconds that passed as they seemed long, but she said nothing still. He could tell that she was thinking of a way to make things even more difficult for him.

"I will tell you on one condition," she told him. Liam didn't let his guard down, not yet.

"What is it?" He asked her.

"We go to the Chief's office and you help me convince him to allow me to move Ash to the ground floor. I need him to be around others like him. I believe it would really help him," she said. Liam was relieved that she had not asked more. He agreed and they got into the elevator and headed for Wellington's office. Looking at her, Liam realised that it was the first time that he had seen her smile in his presence, and it was a beautiful smile. However, it disappeared the moment she caught him staring at her and he looked away.

After convincing Dr. Wellington to let Ash be moved to the ground floor, Liam and Sarah came to the hallway again.

"So where do we talk? We had a deal, remember?" He asked her.

"We cannot talk here. I have to show you," Sarah told him. "Meet me after work hours." With that, Sarah walked away from him and into the elevator.

"Don't worry, Liam McCauley, I don't bite," she said before the doors took her away from his sight.

*I don't bite.* Liam thought on her words again and smiled to himself as he headed for the elevator also. It had been a long time since he had smiled about the unknown

# Chapter Seven

Sarah sat behind her desk staring at nothingness as she tried to wrap her head around the events of the morning. *What just happened?* She asked herself. It seemed unbelievable that the man who had pissed her off the day before and who she was beginning to bear genuine hate for would suddenly take a turnaround and ask for her help. She had looked at him, searched his eyes and he had seemed quite sincere, but what had happened? Sarah wondered still.

However, what puzzled her was the ease with which she had embraced the idea that she might not have to hate Liam anymore. Had she really always wanted to be liked by him? Sarah slapped her cheeks to kill the thought before she got up to go bring Usman out of the ward. She hoped that Usman's testimony and enthusiasm would rub off on Ash and help him also. With her work, the mind was the first to work before the muscles. Everything was connected in a perfect circle and that was what she hoped to show Liam when they met after work.

Her phone rang in the office, which was quite unexpected. No one ever called her. It turned out to be her mother, and she asked to see her as soon as possible.

"Okay mum, but can I know what for? I just got my new job and I can't afford to  miss work," Sarah said after a long silence.

"I know that, but it's very important you come home soon. I have something of great importance to discuss with you. Don't worry, your father will be away, and we will meet in a place where he can't see us, trust me please."

"Okay, I should be home by the weekend, Mum."

Sarah wondered what the problem was now. Sarah still lived her mother and they saw each other occasionally. She sometimes brought Joan with her. Sarah's relationship with her father had been strained since she was a kid, but when he tried to force her into a marriage with Gustavo, it got worse. She despised him and didn't want anything to do with him.

Although he was quite a good father, he was deeply flawed, and his flaws ruined everything. He had always made choices for Sarah and she had never even once liked it. She feels she could have gone very far in life if she had done something else outside the medical  field and not settled for radiology. She sometimes wished she was allowed to be herself. But all of that is gone now, she is now a woman on her own since she went against her father's will and didn't marry Gustavo.

 The time till the end of work seemed longer that day since Sarah kept on checking the clock at intervals so that even Usman had noticed.

"You are cheating on me. That smile on your face, you are thinking of a man," he said to her as she wheeled him around in his wheelchair.

"For one Usman, we are not dating so it is impossible for me to cheat on you," Sarah told him and said nothing more despite his persistence.

Sarah Meyer was a beautiful young woman who knew she was beautiful. She had known since she had won her first beauty pageant at the age of six. However, she had not been with any men. Liam was waiting in her office once they were past work hours. He was as simple looking as he had been in the morning with his jacket slung onto his shoulder.

"So, I am here," he said,

"Good, just do as I tell you. For one, leave your car. We are taking public transport," she told him. For a moment, his brows furrowed as he thought on her words for a while before he eased up and shrugged. Sarah was relieved as they headed out.

Liam was uneasy as they walked past his car and came out of the gates. She had them walk a little distance to a bus-stop where they waited for a bus. Sarah was uneasy as she hoped her plans for the night would not be for naught. They only had to wait about five long silent minutes before they got a bus. They were lucky again to get the seats at the back.

"I think it would be normal for me to ask where you are taking me," Liam finally broke the silence between them.

"Here," she said at first expecting an odd reaction from him but there was none, so she continued. "The one factor that medicine does not factor in is the willpower of each human. While it seems that there is a direct answer for every question, like vomiting equals antibiotics or things like that, they don't put into account the role that the human mind plays in all these. I saw a woman once who was ill and came to a hospital. She had a fever and was given tablets to use but she claimed that they did not work on her. The only thing that worked on her was injections, she claimed. The nurse argued but then a doctor came in. He heard the woman out and then put water in a syringe and injected her with it. Then he told her to go home-"

"Isn't that illegal?" Liam asked just as she had expected him to.

"Perhaps, but the thing is that the woman never came back to the hospital because the fever left her. Now-" She put her left hand on the seat and turned to face him "-the water did not heal her, it was her mind. That is a theory anyways. My point is that medicine can work to a point. I am an Radiologist.  I'm saddled with the responsibility of locating the problem to make it easier to fix the mind first," she told Liam.

"So, you say Liam, it will work if he believes he can?" Liam asked her. It seemed to confuse him.

"I am saying that would make my work easier and increase the chances that it would work," she corrected him.

"So, only Ash can change the outcome of situation in his mind," he said and Sarah nodded before he laughed. "You are crazy, you know that right?" He asked her and Sarah joined him in his laughter.

"A lot of things are possible and there is almost nothing like the impossible. I should not be telling you this because I am your rival," she told him.

"Since when," Liam said shifting closer to her with dare in his eyes. Sarah should have shifted away from him but she could not bring herself to.

"Since you played me at the Award night," she replied to him.

"I apologize for that," he told her sincerely. Thinking about that night, he had remembered her and his sin against her.

"I thrive on competition, so I shall toss aside your apology," she said to him with a wicked smile.

"What a small world then, Sarah Meyer. I thrive on competition too, so you can blink your lovely blue eyes at someone else before they would not make me go any less easy on you," he replied her and for a moment, Sarah covered her face to hide her blush. He pulled her hands off her face to bare her eyes before him again.

"Where are we stopping?" He asked her.

"Yeah, I don't know how far we have gone," Sarah said putting her feet down from the seat and forgetting her hand in Liam's.

"I think I know this area. I have driven past here once before. Have the driver drop us," Liam said as he got to his feet. It was until that moment that

Sarah felt the chill that was the absence of his hands on hers. Neither of them spoke about his hands as they got down from the bus.

"There is a nice restaurant just around the corner where they sell good seafood, do you eat seafood?" Liam asked her. Sarah shrugged.

"I don't know," she said and Liam burst into laughter. Sarah hit him to stop him from mocking her, but her fists did nothing to him.

"Well, for someone so smart, it is sad that you have never eaten sushi. So despite the fact that you are my rival, I shall take you out on a date, Sarah Meyer, just this once and tomorrow, we shall fix Ash," he said to her, offering his hand to her.

Sarah looked at his deep green eyes and saw his truth.

"Okay," she said with a timid shrug as she took his hand.

Liam held her hands and they walked to a nearby seafood restaurant. The place was well lit and from the entrance one could easily spot the kitchen where the steamy delicacies emanated from. A young man pointed to a seat for Liam and Sarah and they both made their way there. Sarah still had her hands locked in between that of Liam and she liked that, but she dared not mention it not even to herself.

At the table Liam brought out his credit card and waved to the waiter to come to their table. He placed an order for the most expensive food on the list despite Sarah protesting it. The duo ate in silence for a while until Sarah asked Liam to say something.

"You did just bring me here to eat right. This is my first date ever so you better not ruin it," Sarah warned jokingly.

"But who said it's a date?" Liam asked with a smirk

"You did Liam, that was what you said, wasn't it? As a matter of fact that's what it is. I don't care what you say," Sarah affirmed.

"Okay okay," Liam said while laughing softly. "I actually brought you here to watch you eat and say some things to you. Make you smile and all," Liam said, looking into Sarah's eyes.

"Okay then. So what are you waiting for? You haven't said a thing to me today, let alone made me laugh."

"Err okay okay, but first I would like to uhm apologise for..." Liam could not finish this sentence before Sarah cut him off.

"You can't you apologise to me? Oh wow!" Sarah said expressing her disbelief and also registering the fact that the almighty Liam was apologising to her, a newbie. The thought of it gladdened her heart and what made her happier was the fact that she would use it to haunt him later.

"Will you let me finish?" Liam snapped. "I want to apologise for how I reacted the other time when you said I looked like someone you knew; I shouldn't have done that," Liam said, slightly showing remorse on his face.

"It's okay now. It's nothing, please let's continue," Sarah said in a bid to remove herself from the awkwardness in the room.

"Yea, we should but the truth is there is a possibility that you used to know me," Liam replied. At the end of his statement Sarah sat down and stared at him for quite a long while, she didn't say or do anything else.

"Wait, why are you staring at me like that?" Liam asked, puzzled.

"What makes that possible Liam, tell me about it and yourself," Sarah said finally.

"Well my life turned a turn when I was around 18 or 19, I guess. Before then all my life I had always been a downtown boy living a simple life, at least according to what I have been told. Turns out I was initially adopted, and my biological parents had been looking for me for the longest time before they found me and that was how my life changed from being a downtown kid to the spoilt brat I am now. I know you most likely think that I'm not a gentleman or well-mannered but what can I do, I was raised this way. It's bad, I know," Liam narrated.

Sarah reached out to touch his hands on the table. "It's okay Liam don't be too hard on yourself; life happens to each and every one of us and we only need to accept the things we cannot change and focus on the ones we can. It must be tough on you to change your family at that age, but it's obvious you also got into a good family, look at you now, a medical doctor."

"Yea, you are right. I try not to think too much about it. Just that sometimes I wonder what I would have been or acted like if my biological parent didn't come for me. And I know this might be somehow weird, I kind of miss the people that adopted me, even though I don't remember much about them."

Liam went on and on about himself. He spoke more about his accident and having been comatose for quite a long time. He recalled being told that he had lost his memory. But he remembered not being part of the McCauleys in his early life. At least Conor made it a duty to always remind him of that. Liam told Sarah how he sometimes felt misplaced and venerable which is why he has chosen to put on a cloak of cockiness to protect himself from the outside world and people.

While he was talking, Sarah sat there and looked at him. Then she mentioned the area where she had met the Liam she knows. On hearing this, Liam looked up to Sarah and touched his head with his hands. His face was obviously grimaced, and Sarah went on to describe Mr. & Mrs. Jameson and how precious their home looked like. Liam then suddenly looked up to Sarah and called her name.

"Sarah, was that you?" Liam asked with a teary eye.

"Yes, I am the one," Sarah said.

The two got up to hug each other. They embraced each other as tightly as possible. It was a really magical moment. Liam started sobbing first and Sarah joined him. They finally broke free when they noticed people in the restaurant were watching and they headed for Liam's house.

Getting into Liam's house, he went into the bathroom loosening the buttons of his shirt as he did. Sarah kicked her shoes off her feet and lay own on the bed waiting.  She later got up and undressed herself near a giant wardrobe. She felt the wet body of Liam meeting with hers from behind as he attempted to unhook her bra strap for her. She could feel his hardness next to her dress. Liam  then used the tip of his tongue to caress her ear, and he proceeded to kiss  her subtly around the neck. Sarah was aroused and her body was already begging for him.

Sarah turned to Liam,   and placed her hand around his neck first, then touched her chin, lifting her face to his, her lips parted gently. His hard dick was now bent upwards, almost touching her belly button. Their duo lips touched each other and they kissed, slowly at first, but passion overtook them and they couldn't stop.

Both Liam and Sarah tried to control themselves but neither of them could. After a while Liam reached for her panties. They were a red thong, and he ran his fingers over the surface for a while, and the feeling of the fabric rubbing against Sarah's vagina made her super wet. He then asked Sarah to take off her panties and she obeyed him. He picked up the red panties and brought them closer to his nose, taking in all its smell before dipping it into Sarah's mouth.

He removed it and Sarah asked him to taste her, so he pushed her violently to the bed and bit her lips subtly with his front teeth. She responded by writhing in both pain and pleasure. He smiled back in satisfaction, and resumed licking and kissing her neck. Sarah begged him to bite her as she enjoyed it, but he refused and teased her instead, pretending to want to bite her, but stopping in between.

Sarah dipped her sharp and long nails into his muscular hard back. Liam got up and Sarah let her fingers run over Liam's body from his neck and collarbone region to his muscular chest and his small but perky nipples and his abs that are as hard as a piece of rock. Sarah then got up and licked them for a while, and a shock of sensation rushed through Liam's body. He clasped his chest to her face as if to force it into his body.

Sarah looked up and gave Liam the perfect seductress smile he personally always craved. Done, Liam dipped his fingers into Sarah's vagina and commented on the tightness. He moved it back and forth slowly in a manner that made Sarah roll her eyes and cause her emerald pupils to disappear. Sarah's legs stiffen as this goes on and she tried to push his hands back, but her body betrayed her in enjoyment.

He then gave Sarah  a taste of herself, as she took his fingers and licked them with a smirking smile. Sarah got wetter due to Liam's comments on her body and the vibration of his voice coming from his chest, which was very close to her and kept driving her crazy, and she didn't want to stop, not any time soon.

Liam  then pressed  Sarah's hand to the bed and sets his dick in between her vagina lips ready to pound her. He kept looking into Sarah's eyes, but his stares means nothing as all she could feel was his hardness and all she could think of was the incoming thrusts. The first thrusts felt somewhat sharp, it lifted her whole body and she came fully alive. Liam then continued to thrust his dick in as far as he could, and as fast as possible, and the bed springs responded rhythmically.

Sarah's  hole couldn't take much more, but she didn't want him to stop either. Liam  stopped suddenly and crawled back towards her legs, letting his face be on her vagina. He moved the tip of his tongue back and forth on her clit in a very fast manner, and Sarah let out a loud moan that satisfied Liam.  Then she covered her mouth with one hand and grabbed Liam's hair with the other, but he yanked her hands off and continued driving his tongue through her vaginal split. Her clitoris was fully swollen by now and he ran his thumb over it.

Liam got up and ran his hands over Sarah's upper body, fondling her breast and nipples making her edgy. He then instructed Sarah to take over as he laid on the bed and tried to catch his breath. Sarah knelt down to stroke his dick, and her touches made his balls tighten. She then rubbed the top of his dick, and each time she did this, Liam felt an electric shock run through his body from his pelvic region.

Sarah licked his dick in a slow and long but stimulating swipe, then took all of Liam into her mouth, her mouth movement making Liam wriggle his waist. Liam used his hand to caress Sarah 's hair, and the passion with which Sarah sucked him reduced.  Liam got up and Sarah stayed below him looking as his body size swallowed her. He held his dick in his hand. Sarah  got  up  and he swept his hand from her back down to her waist.

Her breath was now shaky and unsteady, as Liam bent her over, and gave her a sexy hot spanking that sent both pain and pleasure down Sarah's spine. Then he pounded her with his dick, and she let out soft moans. Liam  grabbed her neck from the back, leaving her in a bent position,  and continued pushing his dick deep into her vagina. Sarah's whole body vibrated along softly, and Liam sped up his thrusts. He finally released into her, pouring all of himself into her. Sweaty and tired, the duo drifts off to sleep in no time like babies.

In the early hours of the next day, Liam woke Sarah up with kisses and breakfast in bed.

"Hey good morning and how was your night?" Liam asked.

"It was fine" Sarah said with a somewhat sad face.

"Sarah? What's wrong" Liam asked, genuinely concerned.

"Nothing, it's just that I don't feel comfortable about what happened between us," Sarah said.

"What was that?" Liam asked pretending not to know what Sarah was talking about.

"What? Are you crazy? You are joking right?" Sarah said red with anger.

"Hey hey relax, I was just joking," Liam said while genuflecting on one of his knees.

"Better, so what are you doing?" Sarah asked, still angry.

"I'm trying to think of a way to ask you to move in with me so I can convince you to spend the rest my life with me," Liam said with a calm and cute face.

Sarah looked at him for a while without saying anything. She felt Liam tense up underneath her because she had remained silent for a while. Then she turned to face him, "well, I might as well spend the rest of my life with you, considering the fact that I have nothing to lose. You know, seeing as I am in love with you and all that jazz."

The look on Liam's face was enough to let her know that she would be happy with him for the rest of her life. He moved over to her side and wrapped her in his arms, kissing her on the forehead then lips before muttering "I love you too." And Sarah knew then that she had found her happily ever after.